This book belongs to

Written by Robert S. Nott.
Illustrated by Lara Ede.

# Bob the BOGEY Fairy

Written by Robert S. Nott · Illustrated by Lara Ede

make
believe
ideas

Fairyland was a place where **all fairies** could follow their dreams and find **fame** and **fortune**. But **not** every fairy was famous.

And in a far, forgotten corner of Fairyland,

beyond the magic dust and wands,

lived one of those fairies.

## His name was Bob.

FAIRY AVENUE

FLUTTER STREET

MAGIC DUST DRIVE

SPARKLE BOULEVARD

BOGEY CANYON

SNOTTY HILLS

Bob

# Bob was the BOGEY Fairy.
It was his job to dispose of the things from your nose!

Bob was the number-one **boGeY** expert in all of Fairyland.

He knew the **difference** between a **Thin 'n' Flaky** and an **Icky-Sticky-Flicky.** Or a **Cluster Chunk** and a **Nose-Snorter.**

He even knew how to deal with a bad case of **Slime-Snizzlers.**

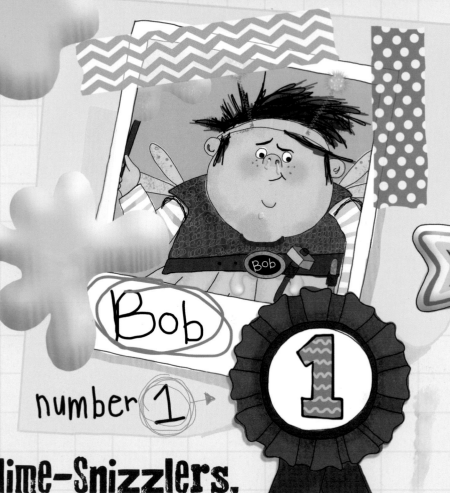

Bob

number 1

# THIN 'N' FLAKY

a super-thin dried nasal mucus that is almost see-through, perfect for fairy-house glazing.

tooth fairy Windows

# ICKY-STICKY-FLICKY

one of those annoying bogeys that no matter how many times you flick...it won't disappear!

colour chart

Morning Pick  Showbiz Smear  Snot Spa  Slime Porridge  Nose Forest  Bogey Breath

# CLUSTER CHUNK

a collection of different-coloured bogeys that have been squeezed and squashed together over a very long time!

# NOSE-SNORTER

a bogey that is easy to locate but super hard to scoop out.

# SLIME-SNIZZLER

a half-bogey, half-slimy-snot that clings like **gloopy** string to the **inside** of your **nose.**

However, being good at his job **wasn't** enough for Bob ...

...he dreamt of being **famous.**

Bob tried everything he could to make his dreams come true, but being the **BOGEY** Fairy didn't help.

"Sorry, you're not as glamorous as the Tooth Fairy."

"I don't think you'd make a very good Fairy Godmother."

"We've decided to go with Tony the Toenail Fairy ... he's got his own scissors."

Then, one day, Bob's luck changed.
While he **chiselled**, **scraped** and **mined**
down the side of **snotty** Simon's bed
(Simon was a secret smearer)...

...something **gleamed** and **glistened** among the
**Cluster Chunks** and the **Icky-Sticky-Flickies.**

It was a tooth!

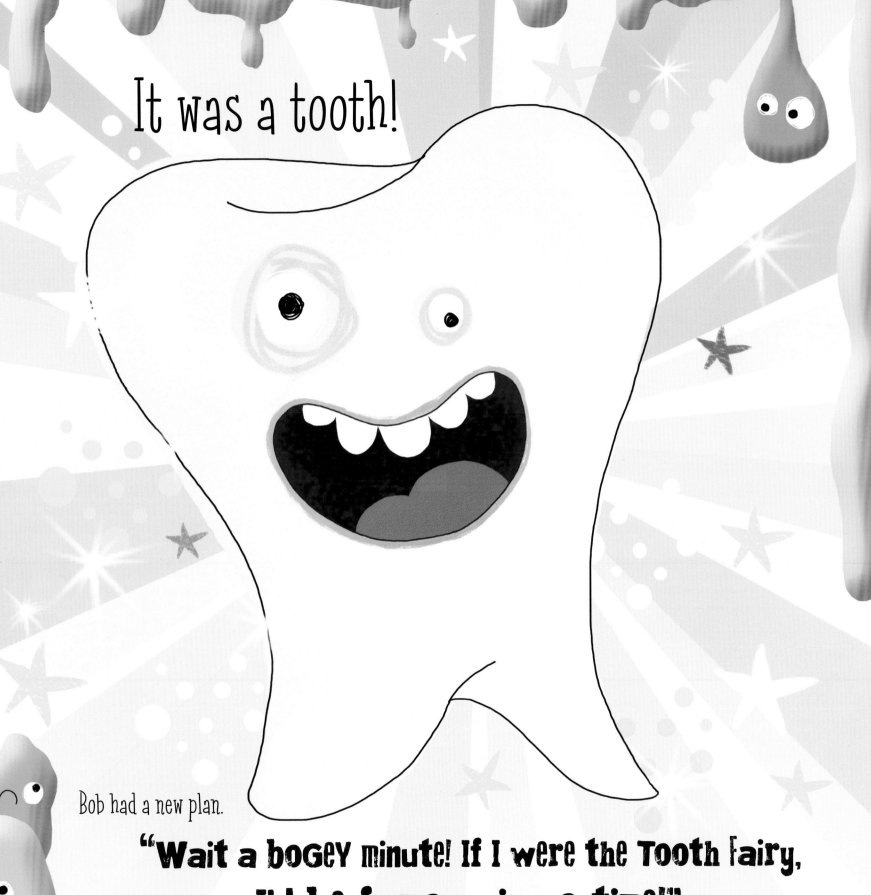

Bob had a new plan.

"**Wait a bogey minute! If I were the Tooth Fairy, I'd be famous in no time!**"

So Bob built a **bogey** trap, tucked Simon's tooth under his pillow and waited silently, until the Tooth Fairy appeared.

Bob burst from the bed … and **flopped** into his own **BOGEY** trap!
The **Tooth Fairy** smiled — she knew exactly what Bob wanted.

"Hmmm, I could do with a rest," she said.
"Do you mind being the Tooth Fairy
for a while?"

Bob didn't hesitate:
**"Absolutely!
I won't let you down."**

However, as morning dawned, the toothless children were in for a **shock.**

For under their pillows, instead of a shiny tooth-fairy coin ...

...there was a
**sticky-icky surprise!**

Bob thought he had done a brilliant job, so you can imagine his reaction when

he saw the Fairyland Star's front page.

**FAIRYLAND STAR**

# WHAT'S HAPPENED TO THE TOOTH FAIRY?

# BOGEYS DISCOVERED... UNDER PILLOWS

# WHO IS THE BOGEY-MAN?

He was finally in the news ... but for all the **wrong** reasons!

Bob fluttered home. His dreams of **fame** and **fortune** had turned into a nightmare.

The **Tooth Fairy** tried to make Bob feel better: "Being famous isn't all it's cracked up to be," she told him. "It's what we do that matters."

"Imagine the mess if the Toenail Fairy didn't clean up everyone's nail clippings.

Or if the Fart Fairy wasn't around to vacuum up all those stinky smells.

And imagine what would happen if you didn't collect all those unwanted bogeys. It would be a..."

...**BOGEY** CATASTROPHE!

# BREAKING NEWS...

## THE WORLD IS BEING OVERRUN BY BOGEYS!

While Bob had been distracted chasing his dreams, people had continued to

**pick and flick,
squidge and roll,
and secretly smear...**

...and with no one to dispose of the things from your nose, the **bogey** mess had grown bigger... and **bigger**... and BIGGER!

"It looks like you have an important job to do!" said the Tooth Fairy.

"You're right! The world needs the BOGEY fairy!" declared Bob.

With his trusted **bogey** wand and a little help from his new friend,

Bob chiselled...

...scraped...

...mined and...

...beat the **bogey catastrophe!**

Everyone gathered for an interview with the **fairy-of-the-moment.**
"Where's Bob the **SUPER-BOGEY** Fairy?" But Bob had fluttered back to Fairyland.

Although Bob wanted to be famous more than anything else, he realised he didn't want to be famous for being

the fairy that had made the **bogey catastrophe** — even if he had saved the day!

Bob now knew he wanted to be famous for doing something **good**.
So with an **epic fairy tale** worth telling...he wrote **this** book!

"I'm FAMOUS!"

BoB's BOOK Signing

(And I hope you'll agree — his story was **bogey-brilliant!**)

THE END